# #PleaseSayYes

A Contemporary Romantic Comedy

Janis,
Thank you
for always making
me feel beautiful!
Hope you enjoy
a little romance!
Love,
Tari Lynn Jewett

by

## Tari Lynn Jewett

# Acknowledgements

There are too many people to thank, and I hope that all of you know how much I appreciate you, and your support in fulfilling my dreams, but I do need to thank a few people, without whose support I would not have made it this far.

Thank you to authors Rebecca Forster and Caitlyn O'Leary, who have held my hand all the way through this process, and occasionally given me a hard shove. To author Joyce Ward, for pushing me to write this story. Thank you to thank my editor, Jenny Jensen for her patience, hard work and positive guidance, my beta readers, Ada Jonnassen, Beverly Strausser, Kandi Ossa, and alpha reader Stephanie Walton, for reading at different stages and great feedback. and when necessary giving me a hard shove. Thank you to my friends at OCC RWA and #CharmedWriters for their incredible support, you have no idea how much you are each loved and appreciated.

And finally thank you to Hunky Hubby aka Paul Jewett and our three sons, Gerrod, Jayson and Joey for always believing in me.

#PleaseSayYes

# Chapter 1

*You've been Framed.* Lucy clicked the notification on her phone. A picture of a skateboard planted in the sand appeared with the message, "@LucySchoolmarm- You know me and I think you're cute. Valentine's is weeks away. I'll be asking you to be my date, but it's not time yet. Until then, #PleaseSayYes #ValentinesIsComing #SecretAdmirer." Lucy read the message again. It was much too early on New Year's morning for cryptic games. She tossed the phone onto the bed and burrowed back under the covers. It was a holiday, she didn't have to be anywhere. She could sleep in as late as she wanted.

Thirty minutes later her ring tone woke her again and she searched the bedcovers for her phone. "Why are you waking me?" she mumbled into the receiver.

"You're still sleeping? So, you didn't see it?" It was Ashley, her best friend and colleague at Beachside Elementary School where she taught fourth grade.

"What? What didn't I see? Why don't you want me to

sleep?" Lucy pushed herself to sit upright and tried to focus her wide blue eyes, she tried to run her fingers through the tangled mass her long, auburn hair had become—New Year's resolution...get a haircut.

"On Framed. You have a secret admirer."

"Oh that. That was real? I thought I was sleeping. I should *be* sleeping." Framed was a social networking app where people could post their photos. Members have a profile and a 'wall' where their pictures and pictures that they are tagged in 'hang' for their followers to see. Other members could comment on photos on your wall. Comments were called 'graffiti'.

"So do you know this guy? I stalked his profile, but there's no picture."

"What's his name?" Lucy reached across the tangle of blankets and fumbled for her tablet sitting on the nightstand.

"TheGuy4U, that's his screen name. His profile just says *musician, skateboarder, beach boy, native Los Angeles South Bay.*"

Lucy rolled onto her back and scrolled down the page until she found the post. "Well, that could be half the guys in the South Bay. Anyway, it's probably spam. I'm sure it's not real."

"Looks real enough to me," Ashley said. "And, wouldn't it be fun if it is real?"

Lucy pushed the heavy covers back, and slid over to

the side of the bed, stretching quickly before answering her friend. "Seriously? It's corny. If he wants to ask me out, why doesn't he just ask me out?" She padded to the kitchen, bare feet barely peeking out of her too long pajama bottoms. She had to make coffee. She couldn't have this conversation without a strong cup.

"I think it's romantic. Imagine he's been watching you from afar." Ashley wove a tale with dramatic flair. "He sees you riding your bike back and forth to school every day, smiles and nods to you, and you nod back automatically. He waits for you to stop and talk to him, but you never do. Finally, he decides to approach you…but how? Should he stop you and ask for your number? Should he leave a note in your bicycle basket when you stop at the market? No, those ideas are too mundane. On New Year's morning, he'll become your secret admirer…on social media for all the world to see."

Lucy waited to be sure her friend was finished before she responded. "I really need to sit in your classroom someday. It must be fun to learn how the pilgrims landed on Plymouth Rock, or to have you discuss the Magna Carta. Do you dress in costume when you do this? I'm taking notes."

"Don't you have a romantic bone in your body?"

"Romance is when a guy breaks his cream filled cookie open and gives you the side with the cream…after he introduces himself, asks you out and takes you on a date.

How does this guy know my name? And that I'm a teacher? He had to know those things to find me, my screen name is Lucy Schoolmarm. I have a stalker."

"Maybe it's that new band teacher Mark Leoni. Have you seen him? He's got great eyes, he's kind of reserved, but I heard him playing the saxophone in the band room after school one day. OMG, I thought I'd melt."

"You just melted because a stranger tagged me in an anonymous post online. I need a mop to clean you up." Lucy considered Mark. "Doesn't Mark have a girlfriend?"

"No, I heard he was engaged, but he caught her cheating with another teacher at his old school, and that's why he moved here from Illinois."

"Where do you hear all of this stuff?"

"If you'd eat your lunch in the teachers' lounge instead of sitting in your classroom with your head in a book…"

Lucy sighed. The teachers' lounge was worse than the quad in high school. There was more gossip, and less than half of it was true.

"Eh, I'm sure it's a onetime thing. I'm not taking it seriously."

"Aren't you going to respond? You should post a picture of yourself on a skateboard, or on your bicycle and tag him."

"Ashley, I don't know him."

"Well, at least reply to his post. Let him know you're interested."

"I'm *not* interested."

"Oh, shoot, gotta' go. Trevor's here. Think about it. I'll talk to Trevor, maybe he can help figure out who it is."

"You do that. I'm going back to bed."

But she didn't. She scooped coffee into the coffee maker, pushed the on button, and headed to the bathroom. She still had a week of winter break left, and she planned on making the most of it.

\*\*\*

She'd had her coffee, showered, sprayed detangler on her hair, brushed out all of the tangles, and graded the last of the kids' California Mission reports. Now, she could work on her fundraising proposal for the new Beachwood Elementary School Library. She smiled at the thought of the project. The current library was outdated, it hadn't been remodeled since the nineteen eighties, and the books hadn't been updated in at least as long. Lucy was hoping to raise enough money to give the library a complete overhaul, add new work stations, stock the shelves with current books, replace badly worn classics and add e-books for the students to check out on their electronic devices. It was going to take a lot of money, and probably two or three years to complete the project, but if she could pull this off, she'd feel like she had made an important difference at her school.

She checked her phone for messages and there were eighteen notifications on Framed. Great, eighteen of her friends and followers were encouraging this idiot. According to Framed, the account had been created at two a.m. this morning. Oh, now she got it, he was drunk and at a New Year's Eve party when he did this, probably on a dare from his friends, and he probably wouldn't even remember what he'd done tomorrow when his hangover wore off. Anyway, he wasn't following anyone else, just her, but he already had thirty-two followers and his only post was the photo of the skateboard standing up in the sand...with eighteen comments below it.

"@TheGuy4U and @LucySchoolmarm, will your first date be on a skateboard?"

"@TheGuy4U, do you live at the beach? Work at the beach? Or just play at the beach?"

"@LucySchoolmarm, time to get your head out of the books and go on a date." From @AshleyBeachrunner ...her best friend of course.

"@LucySchoolmarm, I think you're cute too, will you go out with me? -@HermosaSurfer."

"@TheGuy4U sick board Dude! You gotta' be a real ripper with wheels like that!"

And the comments continued, some directed to Lucy, some to TheGuy4U. Lucy shook her head and sighed. It had to be a prank. She picked up the television remote and turned on Channel Five. Perfect, she could watch the replays of the Rose Parade and make herself some lunch.

# Chapter 2

Evan was going to be ticked off when he found out about this, unless it worked…hmmm, maybe especially if it worked. But Kyle was tired of watching his younger brother mope around on Saturday nights when all of the other guys in the band had girlfriends supporting them. Last night, New Year's Eve at Beach Break Coffee Bar, which they owned together, was the worst. All of their friends were at the coffee bar, dancing, laughing, most were coupled up, and between sets, Evan sat at a table alone morosely nursing a beer. The Pipeline, their band, ended their last set at eleven p.m. because of a local noise ordinance, and Evan didn't even wait to toast the New Year in before going upstairs to the apartment the two brothers shared over the coffee bar.

Kyle was sick of it and when his friends, Doug and Carrie, started talking about how they'd met online, Kyle got an idea. He already knew the perfect girl for Evan, he just couldn't get Evan to talk to her. He'd hook them up online. When everyone had left the party, he'd logged onto the computer and created an anonymous account on Framed. Using a picture he'd found of Evan's skateboard pitched in the sand, he'd tagged the cute little schoolteacher who came into the coffee bar every morning—and sometimes again in the evening—for a hazelnut latte with almond milk.

That was twelve hours ago. The coffee bar was closed today for the holiday. Kyle finally dragged himself out of bed, and when he checked his phone, there were twenty-seven comments graffitied on the anonymous post, but not one from Lucy. Her friends were egging her on though, so he'd post another picture tomorrow morning. He just had to figure out what to post…and what he would post for the next forty days…and how he was going to tell Evan if she said yes.

# Chapter 3

"You've been Framed by @TheGuy4U." Lucy read the notification when she got out of the shower on Tuesday morning. Really? So, this guy was on a New Year's bender. She clicked on the notification to see what he'd posted today.

A silhouetted picture of a guy playing guitar on the beach was hung on her wall with a message graffitied below.

"@LucySchoolmarm. Before you say yes to anyone else for a Valentine's date, I thought we should get to know each other better. I love music, and play several instruments. I started with drums at eight years old. Do you play an instrument or sing? Or are you a music fan? #PleaseSayYes #ValentinesIsComing #SecretAdmirer #GettingToKnowYou.

She had to admit the picture was pretty hot. Just a guy with longish hair, standing on the beach with his guitar, silhouetted by an amazing sunset. She tried to figure out who it was, but the picture could have been so many guys. For all she knew, it wasn't even TheGuy4U. She put the phone on the bathroom counter and rubbed herself dry with the soft terry towel.

Was it someone from school? Or maybe a neighbor? She lived in a studio apartment right on The Strand. It was crazy high rent, but she didn't need a car. She was three blocks from Beachside Elementary, and rode her bike just about everywhere else she needed to go. Maybe it was the head lifeguard at the pier. He was pretty hunky in his red lifeguard shorts. No, it couldn't be Freddie, the profile…if it was to be believed, said the guy was a business owner. Did she know any business owners? There was her landlord, but he was in his mid-sixties and had been married for nearly forty years. There was the guy who owned the surfboard shop on Pier Avenue. Hey, and he sold skateboards in there, but then again so did the guy at the bicycle shop on Pacific Coast Highway, although he was married with two small children.

She put on a long sleeve tee, then stepped into a pair of jeans, hopped up and down and wiggled until they were comfortably situated. She didn't think it could be any of the single guys at school, well…either of the single guys at school, since there were only five male staff members and three were married. That left the new band director and the school psychologist, and she was pretty sure neither of them owned a business, and although the band director made Ashley melt when he played the sax, and could possibly be the guy in the picture, he wasn't a South Bay native. No, her colleagues were out.

She pulled her hair into a ponytail, and slipped on a pair of shoes to run down to Beach Break Coffee Bar for her morning latte.

\*\*\*

The coffee bar was still quiet. It was only eight-thirty, and most people were either at work or out taking advantage of holiday sales. She sat in a window seat, sipped her hazelnut latte and broke pieces from her oatmeal cranberry muffin to dunk into the cardboard cup. The Beach Break Coffee Bar had a real beach feel, surfboards signed by surfing legends through the ages hung on the walls between windows. Autographed photos of world class surfers were scattered on the back walls and on the walls behind the counter. The floors were a sandy beige, and the walls were painted a turquoisey blue. They served baked goods, sandwiches, small gourmet plates of appetizers and finger foods, but were known for their specialty coffee, locally brewed beer and selection of fine California wines. This was Lucy's haven, her favorite place for a beverage and a good book.

She tapped on her phone. Eighty-two people had

'liked' the second post by TheGuy4U, and twenty-four had commented.

"@LucySchoolmarm, are you going to say yes?"

"@TheGuy4U, what's the name of your band?"

"@TheGuy4U, what if she doesn't play an instrument?"

"@LucySchoolmarm, well? Do you play an instrument or sing?"

And they went on.

Lucy stared at the phone. Really people, don't you have anything better to do? She pulled a book from her bag and opened it. Before she knew it, she was lost in the late eighteen-nineties in someone else's love story.

\*\*\*

Behind the counter, Evan took inventory of the various coffee beans the coffee bar stocked, and tallied them so that he could place their order. Next would be beers and wines. Every now and then he looked across the room to Lucy. She was so pretty. It didn't matter whether she was dressed for school, dressed for a night out with her friends, or in a tee shirt and jeans, she was beautiful. Today she didn't have a drop of make-up on, but those big blue eyes with her long dark lashes really drew him in. He should go over and talk to her, but what would he say? 'Nice weather, huh?' Or 'How's the latte?' No, he'd just finish his order... Jamaican java, hazelnut heaven, salt caramel mocha...

\*\*\*

Lucy finished her muffin as she read her book. For Christmas, she'd received the latest release by her favorite author of Victorian romance and now that the mission grades had been entered into the computer she could indulge. Victorian romance was her guilty pleasure.

She'd only gotten through twelve pages when her thoughts distracted her. Maybe the guy was a regular at the Beach Break Coffee Bar. She was here every morning before school, and most weekend mornings. She looked around the coffee shop, the place was beginning to fill up. There was the realtor guy, talking on his cell phone, a couple making googly eyes at their baby—no single men she recognized. Oh, there was the guy who lived two doors down from her. What was his name? David? Daniel? She couldn't remember. He was kind of cute. His hair was short, and the guy in the picture had longish hair, but he may have cut it. She didn't know if he owned a business, played guitar or was a South Bay native. All she knew about him was that he lived two doors down from her. He lived there already when she moved in. He was quiet but neighborly, nodding at her whenever they saw each other. Patrick! That was his name.

She picked up her phone, there were thirty-two new comments on The Guy4U's post, and it was eleven-thirty. She dropped her book back into her purse. Why was she letting this distract her? She pushed in her chair and waved goodbye to the two brothers who ran the Beach Break.

"See you tomorrow," Kyle called to her.

"Bright and early," she answered smiling.

# Chapter 4

*You've been Framed by @TheGuy4U*. Lucy was thirty-seven pages into her new book when the notification sounded on her tablet. Seriously? It was one a.m. She pushed the tablet off her nightstand and into the top drawer, slamming the drawer shut. Now, where was she? Lady Everly had just slapped the rogue Lord of the Manor and was about to tell him what she thought of him. Lucy glanced toward the top drawer. Should she be scared? Or was this harmless? She wasn't going to look. She rolled to her side, back facing the nightstand with the offending tablet and went back to page thirty-seven.

"Lady Everly flounced up the stairs leaving Lord—" It wouldn't hurt to look.

She put the book down and rolled to the other side, retrieving her tablet from the drawer and tapping the Framed app. Up popped a picture of a male fishing on the pier. The picture was taken from the back. His head covered with a hat, sitting on a beach chair leaning forward as he reeled his catch in. The caption said, *@LucySchoolmarm I hope you like halibut. #pleasesayyes #valentinesiscoming #secretadmirer #gettingtoknowyou*

There were already seventy-eight comments graffitied under the photo.

"@TheGuy4U what did you catch?"

"@TheGuy4U this is so romantic. I wish I had a secret admirer."

"@LucySchoolmarm are you out there?"

And the graffiti comments went on from there. @TheGuy4U already had over two hundred followers, and it was barely day three of the new year. She pulled up a blank page on her tablet and started to type a list of all of the single men she could think of. Then she typed a small checkmark next to those she could eliminate. There weren't many left, and none of them seemed right. Oh, well, she turned off the bedside lamp and pulled up the blankets. She was having lunch with Ashley later today, maybe she could help her.

\*\*\*

"You beat me here! Usually I'm into my second glass of wine, and I've eaten most of the bread in the basket before you show up." Ashley slid into the booth across from Lucy and grabbed the glass of wine in front of Lucy for a sip. "You could have ordered a glass of wine for me too."

"I didn't know what you wanted," Lucy said, finally looking up from her e-tablet. "You never order the same thing twice."

"You, however, are very predictable. A glass of Pinot Grigio. No matter what time it is, or what you're eating, it's Pinot Grigio for Lucy."

"And why not? It's like the little black dress, versatile and classic."

"So what are you reading? You must have been reading since you were sitting here early."

"Actually, I wasn't." Lucy tapped her tablet and handed it to Ashley just as their server arrived.

"Are you ready to order? Or should I give you a few more minutes?"

They placed their orders, Lucy her standard grilled chicken salad, Ashley throwing caution to the wind and ordering the chef's special, crispy wok fried whole fish with a garlic butter sauce. Sometimes Lucy wished she could be as spontaneous as Ashley, but she liked the comfort of a routine.

Ashley handed the tablet back to Lucy as the server left. "Screen went black, what did you want to show me?"

Lucy held her thumb to the home button and handed the device back to Ashley. "I've made a list of all of the single men that I can think of, those with a check beside their name have already been disqualified. And the few that are left just don't seem like possibilities. Any ideas?"

Ashley smiled as she perused the list. "So you are interested! No not this guy…or this one…So why haven't you responded to his posts? You have to let him know you're interested." Ashley started typing on the pad.

"I can't respond until I know who it is—what are you doing?"

"Adding a few names to your list. See what you think." She handed the tablet back to Lucy.

"Oh my gosh, I didn't think about Bill at the Marine Animal Hospital. He was so good with the kids when we took them for a field trip. I wonder if he's a musician? And Faheem who owns the trampoline gymnasium, he *is* a musician, he plays guitar in a band that performs at the Saloon once a month. Brandon, is that the guy I met at your New Year's party?"

"No that was Josh, add him to the list. Brandon is the tech guy who created the new homework forum for kids to get after school help online."

"Okay, he owns his own business, but is he a native of the South Bay? And is he a musician?" Lucy asked.

Ashley pulled out her phone and started typing. "Well, the only way to find out is to do our own online stalking."

By the time the girls had finished their lunch and two more glasses of wine they had added a dozen more names, and eliminated half as many. The list was growing, and they were going to have to do some serious reconnaissance.

After lunch the girls went for a mani-pedi at Mermaid Scales and Pretty Nails, a skin and nail salon.

"You have to respond, Lucy. We need to make a plan of attack," Ashley insisted as a manicurist dipped each of their feet in the hot wax, then dipped again.

"I don't want to respond until I know who he is. What if he's some loser who's just trying to get into my pants?"

"What if he's Prince Charming and some other Princess squeezes her foot into your glass slipper?" Ashley scrolled through her phone while the manicurist worked on her feet. "Listen to this…@*TheGuy4U if @LucySchoolmarm isn't interested in meeting you, I'll say yes. #pleasesayyes #valentinesiscoming #thegirl4U*. And then there's this message from @BrownEyedGirl, @*TheGuy4U LucySchoolmarm isn't the only teacher in town, just sayin' #pleasesayyes #teachersdoitwithclass*. You have to respond."

"Look, if he's willing to take up with just any online tramp, then I'm not the girl for him anyway."

"You realize he's up to over three hundred followers already."

"Really? That's another hundred since this morning. This is so surreal."

"We have to plan some responses, and some pictures to Frame him in."

"OMG Ashley, you're making me nervous."

"Look, I've watched you crawl further and further into your shell since Cory broke things off and left for Australia. It's been long enough, and I'm glad to see someone giving you some attention. Don't worry, we'll make sure this guy is okay, but for now a little internet flirtation couldn't hurt."

Lucy sighed. Her friend was right. Since Cory had packed up his things and left for a job in Australia she'd primarily focused on her job and kept her social life to lunches and movies with girlfriends. She'd avoided girls' nights out at bars, and even parties where her friends might try to set her up. She'd only gone to Ashley's New Year's Eve party because Ashley was her best friend. Cory had been gone over a year. Maybe it was time to get out, but she'd probably be better off letting her friends set her up on a blind date than letting the internet do it.

# Chapter 5

The Coffee Bar closed at midnight on weekdays. Kyle did closings and Evan opened, so Kyle was often working until one a.m. or later, and had the place to himself if he wanted to stay up for a little while. He sat at the computer looking at the posts he'd already made, staring in disbelief at the number of people following and commenting on his little set up. So far the only people not participating seemed to be the two who were targeted—Evan and Lucy. He had to come up with something good for his next post, some way to get her to respond. He didn't want to be creepy or stalkerish…although, the stalker boat may have already sailed, but he wanted to let her know that he, well, Evan, knew her enough to genuinely like her.

*Crash, BANG, Clink, bang.* Kyle jumped out of his seat, and headed toward the back door to look into the back-parking lot, grabbing a baseball bat that he kept near the exit just 'in case.' He opened the back door, leaving the security screen door locked and peered into the deserted lot, lit only dimly by the lights out on the street. A shadow raced past him…RRRowww. It was just one of the neighborhood feral cats. A metal can was still rolling down the row of empty parking spaces. She must have knocked it off of one of the fire escapes. He locked the door and headed back to the office and his task.

"What the heck is this?" Evan was sitting at the computer, staring at the screen. "Who's @TheGuy4U? And why is there a picture of my skateboard? The picture of me playing guitar on the beach? And the picture of me fishing?"

"I—uh."

"Who's @LucySchoolmarm? Is that Lucy? Hazelnut Latte, with a pinch of nutmeg and the crooked smile Lucy? What have you done?" Evan demanded.

"I—uh."

"You already said that, Kyle. Try something new, whole words, and make sentences."

"Well, you like her and I think she likes you, so I thought…maybe…"

"You thought, maybe…you'd pretend to be me? You'd ask her out for me because I'm too lame to ask her out myself? That it?"

Kyle hung his head. He'd known he was crossing the line, but he'd hoped that by the time Evan found out, it would be too late, and he'd already have a date with Lucy.

Looked like it wasn't going to happen.

"Does she know? Does she know it's me?"

"I don't think so. She hasn't responded. But…"

"Oh, great, she probably thinks I'm a total jerk. Couldn't ask her out in person, so I stalk her on the internet instead."

"Look at all of the comments, Evan. The guys are all cheering you on, and the girls are either cheering you on or asking you out. They all think it's romantic. Read it; there are hundreds of comments on the pictures. It's just the three you saw, and look at all of the followers in just three days. People like seeing love bloom."

"But it's not love. It's you, you alone…" but Evan had turned back to the computer and was reading.

"I'll remove it all in the morning if you want. I'm going to bed," Kyle told his brother. Evan's only response was a grunt.

Lucy put a marker in her romance novel. It was the end of the chapter—a good place to stop. It was after one a.m. She'd check her social media quickly before going to bed. Hmmm, lots of new responses to @TheGuy4U's previous posts, but no new post from him. Not that she cared. She really wasn't interested. She decided to read just one more chapter.

At two a.m., she checked again. She was tagged in a Christmas photo by her sister-in-law. She skimmed through holiday photos other friends had posted and graffitied on some of their walls, but there was nothing new from @TheGuy4U. Was she disappointed?

She turned on the television and looked for a late-night movie. Seriously, "You've Got Mail"? But, she set the timer and snuggled up to watch until she drifted off to sleep.

# Chapter 6

Evan tried not to stare at Lucy sitting at her favorite table by the window, stirring her latte and breaking off pieces of the double fudge brownie she'd ordered instead of her usually healthy muffin. He was so embarrassed by what his brother had done that he'd barely spoken to her when he took her order. She hadn't seemed like she was in the mood to talk either, although now she was on the phone having a very animated conversation.

"I know you told me to respond to his posts, but I don't know what to say." Then a pause.

"I did say it didn't matter to me." Another pause.

"I'm sure it was just a big joke. Some guy is sitting with his buddies having a good laugh over this." Lucy looked pensive as she listened to the response.

"I know, but I was just starting to like it. I mean…well, it was kind of sweet."

Evan hated that he was eavesdropping, but could it be that she was talking about her online secret admirer? Was she disappointed that he…er, Kyle, hadn't posted today?

"Yes, of course I'm drowning my sorrows in chocolate. Tomorrow, wait, tomorrow is Friday, right? That sounds good. I could use a night out. Okay, I'll talk to you later. Bye, Ash."

Evan got back to work cleaning imaginary fingerprints on the glass pastry case. Hmmm, he thought, Kyle's idea seemed to have, at the very least, intrigued her. Should he do something? He could simply walk over and talk to her. He turned back around just in time to see her open the door.

"Bye Evan, see you tomorrow!" she said brightly as she walked out.

Evan waved as the door closed behind her. He'd ask her out tomorrow, that would give him time to think of something clever…or at least intelligent to say.

But he didn't. Three days went by, and each day he took her morning order for a latte and a muffin. Each night he checked *Framed* for graffiti on the @TheGuy4U wall—he didn't consider it his wall, and was stunned by the number of people who were invested in the posts, but there were no comments from Lucy. He knew, however that Lucy was checking her *Framed* wall for new posts. He'd overheard a couple of cell phone conversations discussing the subject.

Kyle tried to talk to him a couple of times when their

shifts overlapped. But Evan just grunted. He was really ticked off that Kyle had put him in this position. And yet...

\*\*\*

Monday morning Lucy arrived at school bright and early, ready to inspire young imaginations. The morning flew by quickly, her students excited to do art projects inspired by their holiday breaks. She'd get back into the heavier work, math, science and verb tenses in a few days, after the kids had calmed back down.

Lunchtime came around and Lucy started to get comfortable at her desk, pulling out a new novel and her putting her lunchbox on the table. But as she flipped the latch on her lunchbox she stopped. Maybe she should go to the teachers' lounge. She could read at home when she ate dinner. Ashley had spent Friday night badgering her about her anti-social behavior. Maybe the teachers' lounge would be a good start. She put her book in her top desk drawer, closed the latch on her lunchbox and headed to the lounge.

She regretted her decision the minute she crossed the threshold.

"Hey, look everyone! It's LucySchoolmarm," Juan Torrez, the sixth-grade science teacher called out. "So how come you haven't said 'yes' to TheGuy4U?"

"Yeah, Lucy. He said please and everything," said Melissa, one of the second-grade teachers. "Say yes, or at least respond to him so he doesn't give up."

Lucy turned around to retreat just in time to be shoved right back in by Ashley.

"Leave her alone, you idiots! I've just about gotten her to come around, and you're going to undo all of my hard work," Ashley reprimanded the room as she led Lucy to a long lunch table and pushed her into a chair. "Sit."

"My, you're bossy," Lucy said.

"Whatever it takes Luce."

Lucy's phone dinged. She pulled it out of her sweater pocket in unison with several of her colleagues. *You've been Framed by @TheGuy4U.* And everyone in the room started talking at her again. The photo was a picture of Lucy's blue beach cruiser bicycle leaned against one of the posts on the pier. The wicker basket attached to the front of her bike was filled with books. She remembered that day, it was last October. The caption read, *I had to take this picture of your beach cruiser and books, it was so you. No, I'm not stalking you, but our paths do cross often. #pleasesayyes #bikesandbooks #valentinesiscoming #secretadmirer.*

On that day, there had been a big sale at her favorite store, The Either Or Bookstore, one block up the hill on Pier Avenue. How did someone get a picture of her bike and books without her knowing it? Should she be worried? Was this guy more a stalker than secret admirer?

In the lunchroom, all of her colleagues were talking at once, firing questions her way.

"So you have to respond, Lucy! We thought he'd given up on you, give him something."

"No, play it cool. Make him work for it."

"You are going to say yes, aren't you?"

"Do you have any idea who it is?"

Lucy could feel anxiety building and she started looking around for an escape, but Ashley put a calming hand on her arm. "People, inside voices. You're scaring poor Lucy," Ashley said in her firmest teacher voice. But the group was already riled up. Ashley rose from her seat and banged the plastic bowl that held her salad on the table. "I will remove Lucy from this room if I have to." She waited for the voices to fade away. "Thank you. Now maybe we can give her a little support and help her decide on an action plan.

For the rest of the lunch break the tight knit group of educators pored over all of the posts that *TheGuy4U* had made and made a list of clues as to his identity. He was a Los Angeles South Bay native, he was a musician, he owned a business, he rode a skateboard, he fished, he either lived or worked near the pier area, or maybe both, he had slightly longish hair but they couldn't tell the color from either picture of him. There was also no clue as to the kind of business that he owned, it could be fishing or beach related, or he could be an insurance salesman for all they knew.

When the first bell rang signifying that the kids should line up on the playground, and teachers should return to their classrooms, Lucy was overwhelmed, but she also felt a nice warmth—her friends were taking care of her.

# Chapter 7

"Chicken taco salad without the tortilla chips and I'll just have the salsa as dressing, and a diet cola," Ashley told the server at lunch on Saturday.

"No margarita or tortilla chips?" Lucy asked her after the server had left.

"No, I gained six pounds over the holidays, and I want to get it off before Valentine's…which is only five weeks away you know," Ashley said pointedly.

"I know. I still don't know what I should do."

"Well, you should at least respond to him."

"I don't know what to say."

"Answer one of his questions, or ask him one of the questions on that list we made in the teachers' lounge yesterday. Start making him reveal himself."

"But what if it's someone I'm not attracted to? I don't want to lead him on."

"Just ask him some questions, we'll work on it from there."

Lucy half nodded, half shook her head in agreement.

"Trimmed down taco salad?" A different server brought their meals. Ashley raised her hand and the server set the plate down in front of her. "So the super deluxe burrito with everything on it must be for you." The server looked at Lucy as she put the plate in front of her. Lucy had the good grace to drop her head in shame. She'd never had to worry about her weight, and occasionally when her friends had to work so hard to stay in shape while it just seemed to come naturally for her, she did feel a bit guilty.

"Sorry, Ash," Lucy said." I could have ordered something a little less…well, just less."

"Don't worry about it, Lucy. I've been dieting since I was twelve. It doesn't even bother me anymore, in fact sometimes it just makes me feel righteous." She picked up her fork and dove into the salad.

Lucy waited a minute before picking up her fork.

"And what's making this easier, is I'm going to make you walk across the promenade with me to Randi's Rags to try on some dresses."

"Okay, we can do that. What are you guys doing for Valentine's?"

"I'm not sure yet, but whatever it is, I'll be wearing a sexy new dress and some cute new shoes."

Lucy laughed. "Trevor better bring his 'A' game then."

***

"Hi, ladies, haven't seen you two since New Year's Eve! What a great party, Ashley. thanks again for inviting us," Randi, the owner of the little beach boutique and a friend, greeted them.

"I'm so glad you and Colin came," Ashley said. "It was a great night."

"We had a blast. Can I get you something to drink? Soda? Water?"

"No, no, this isn't a social call, we're actually here to spend money. I'm looking for a dress for Valentine's, and then of course, Lucy might need one too."

Lucy had known Randi since they'd attended elementary school at Beachside, and neither had had any desire to wander very far. Ashley and Lucy had met as student teachers at Beachside, and had become good friends from the start. By the time they'd found out that both of them had been hired as full time teachers at Beachside, the three girls had formed a tight knit group.

"Oh, really? What have I missed since New Year's?"

"You haven't seen what's going on on *Framed?*" Ashley asked while Lucy shifted uncomfortably from one foot to the other.

"No, my New Year's resolution was to spend less time on social media. What did I miss?'

"You picked the wrong time to go on a social media

diet." Ashley pulled out her phone. "Lucy here has a secret admirer on *Framed.*" She handed the phone to Randi and showed her the posts from *TheGuy4U*. Randi scrolled through the photos and comments.

"She hasn't responded to his posts," Ashley said. Lucy still hadn't said a word.

"Do you have any idea who it is?" Randi asked, looking at Lucy as she handed the phone back to Ashley.

"Not a clue. We know he's a local guy, he owns a business, and he's a musician. Just enough to pique my interest, but not enough to tell me who he is," Lucy said, finally getting a word into the conversation about her.

Ashley had started looking through the racks of new clothing that Randi had put up since the holidays. Some of the garments were designed by Randi and some were exclusive purchases. Everything in the store was special.

"What do you have that's sensuous, but not blatantly sexy?" Ashley asked.

"Really Ash? Let's see, something to go with your blonde hair and…"

"Oh no! Not for me, I'm going full out sex kitten, something like this little red number." She held the dress up by the hanger so they could see. "Low back, short skirt, skin tight to hug all of my curves. But Lucy, wouldn't be brave enough for this, so something romantic, but understated."

"That sounds right," Randi said with a laugh. "And, I

think I have just the thing for you Lucy." She headed to the stockroom.

"But I don't even know if I'm going out with this guy."

"That's okay, just try it on."

"I'm taking this one into the dressing room, Randi. Oh, and this one too." Ashley hooked another daring red dress off a rack.

Lucy slid hangers across the racks admiring new fashions that had come in. There was always something new and different in Randi's store. Randi had a real eye for style.

"I designed this myself, and the dresses came in this morning," Randi said holding up a darling little black dress with clean feminine lines, classically cut with an Audrey Hepburn feel to it. "I think it would look great on you. Try it on."

"Oh, it's so cute, but I don't even know who this guy is. I'm not…"

"Just try on the dress, whether you wear it for Valentine's or some other time, I know it will be perfect for you."

Lucy looked the dress up and down. It really was cute. "Alright, but I'm just trying it on." She grabbed another dress off the rack she'd been perusing and took them both to a dressing room.

The door to Ashley's dressing room squeaked open

and she stood in the doorway wearing the steamy hot dress. The dress clung from shoulder to mid-thigh. The low-cut front draped down to her midriff, and hugged her hips. She turned around so that Lucy could see the back, which was lower cut than the front, dipping dangerously close to the dimples above her backside.

"Well, if that doesn't make Trevor feel romantic, I don't know what will," Lucy said from the open stall across from Ashley.

"Right? He better make this a special Valentine's if he wants his gift."

"What are you getting him?"

Ashley rolled her eyes. "This dress of course. Let me see when you've got the dress on, Luce." Ashley closed the door, but Lucy could hear her clearly from the other side. "Dang, I'm hot." Lucy shook her head smiling.

First Lucy tried on the dress she'd grabbed from the rack. It was adorable, a black fitted bodice, with a full fifties style skirt with sheer fluffy layers. She really liked it. She looked at the tag, well, she wasn't sure she liked it *that* much. Although, she knew Randi would give her a 'friend' discount.

"Come on let me see," Ashley called to her from the other side of the door.

"Alright, alright." Lucy opened the door and spun in a circle making the skirt float around her.

"Really cute. Is that the one Randi picked for you?"

Lucy shook her head. "No, I picked this one."

Ashley took out her phone and took a couple of pictures. "Try on the other one," Ashley ordered.

"Yes, ma'am." Lucy turned and shut the door behind her.

From the minute, she slipped the little black dress over her head, she knew she had to have it. The dress was sleeveless with wide set shoulders that showed off her creamy skin and delicate neck, and it fit her perfectly without being tight or clingy. It hugged her hips, gently accentuated her delicate curves and was so classic and feminine. The back came down to just above her bra strap showing skin, without being as dangerously showy as the dress that Ashley had found. Of course, Ashley had been with Trevor for several years now, and Lucy didn't even know TheGuy4U.

"What are you doing in there? I want to see." Ashley banged on the door.

"Okay, okay." She slid the door latch and opened the door.

"That's it, that's the one," Ashley said. Randi stood next to her smiling and pleased with herself.

"Hold up your hair."

Lucy pulled her hair back, twisted it and held it up on her head with one hand.

"I knew that was the dress for you!" Randi said as she reached over and tucked the tag down in back.

"TheDress4U to wear for TheGuy4U on Valentine's," Ashley quipped.

"I don't know if I'm going out with him, but I love this dress. How much Randi?"

"It's on special just for you."

Ashley took out her phone and took a couple more pictures. "Turn around, Lucy." Lucy did a fashion model turn and looked back over her shoulder toward Ashley.

"Thank you, Randi. I love the dress and appreciate the discount," Lucy said.

"You had to have this dress, it looks amazing on you." Randi slipped a plastic garment cover over Lucy's little black dress before handing it to her.

Valentine's was still weeks away, and Lucy had a dress, but she wasn't sure about the date.

# Chapter 8

The January ocean air was brisk and Lucy pulled her jacket tight around her. It was cold for Hermosa Beach. The sign on the lifeguard stand said the air temperature was fifty-six degrees and the water temperature was fifty-eight! The girls walked two doors down to the Beach Break Coffee Bar talking the whole time.

"I'd like a pomegranate tea, and one of those delicious…" Ashley stopped and looked down at the garment bag hanging over her arm. "Just the tea please."

"A hazelnut latte and one of those chocolate dipped biscotti cookies, please." Lucy winked at Evan making him blush as he took her order.

Ashley smacked her arm.

"Hey that stung!" Lucy said laughing.

"You're so mean. You know I can't eat anything bad if I want to fit into this dress."

"I didn't buy it; you did! And anyway, at the restaurant you told me it didn't bother you."

"Well, when it comes to chocolate, it does bother me."

They sat down at a window table.

"Okay, so how are you going to respond to TheGuy4U? It's time."

"I don't know what to say. And maybe I shouldn't respond, he's a total stranger."

"You don't know that, it sounds like he knows you, and what can he do with everyone in the South Bay Beach cities watching. Have you seen how many people are following now? He'd be suspect number one."

Both girls took out their phones at the same time, pulling up the Framed website.

"Seriously? There are more than twelve hundred people following him now? All he's done is post four photos!"

"It's time to respond," Ashley pushed.

"I don't know."

"I have an idea." Ashley's fingers raced across her phone while Lucy watched.

"What are you doing?"

"Don't worry, this will get things going… And done."

Lucy tapped her phone, her grip tightened on the device in her hand, and she felt her stomach turn. "NO, what have you done?"

Ashley just smiled. Neither girl noticed that across the room Evan was also looking at his phone and smiling.

***

The dress was shoved into the back of the closet, and Lucy was curled up in bed with a large glass of Pinot Grigio and the romance she'd been trying to read since New Year's, a historical romance by her favorite author, the perfect distraction. She adjusted her pillows, and sank into the warm blankets, but just as she was about to open her book, her phone binged telling her that she had a new text message. It was Ashley.

*You can't be mad at me. My post has gone crazy and ThatGuy4U responded.*

Lucy typed back. *I can be mad at you!*

But, she clicked on the Framed app and Ashley's icon. No way. Ashley had posted pictures of Lucy posing in the dressing room of Randi's Rags in each of the dresses she'd tried on. Three hundred and forty-three people had voted, almost overwhelmingly for the dress that Lucy had purchased. She scanned the graffiti under the photos. There it was.

*Lucy is beautiful in anything she wears. You can dress in sweats if you want to, just say yes, but if I'm going to pick one, I pick #dress2 #justsayyes #valentinesiscoming. @TheGuy4U.*

Lucy smiled. Who was this guy? She wanted to know before she said yes, but she just might have to say yes to find out!

***

Randi ran along The Strand every morning before opening the store. She put her left foot up on the low wall that separated the sand from sidewalk and stretched out her legs. She didn't usually do warm up exercises, she liked to just take off running, but she was stalling and just as she switched feet to stretch the other side...

"Good morning, Randi. Late run today?" Kyle asked.

Randi turned around and they took off running together. "I was kind of waiting for you."

"Is that so?"

"Lucy and Ashley came by to do some shopping on Saturday."

"And you wanted to tell me that you're now independently wealthy?"

Randi laughed. "No, it's what they told me." They both kept their focus straight ahead as they ran, nodding periodically at other morning regulars. "Did you know that Lucy has a secret admirer on Framed?"

"No kidding?"

"Come on, you had to know. Apparently most of the South Bay knows about this."

"Is that so?" Kyle picked up speed and Randi kicked it in gear to keep up.

"I know that it's Evan. I recognized the picture of him with his guitar on the beach. I was there when the photo was taken."

Kyle slowed to a more comfortable step. "Shoot, I didn't expect this thing to get so out of hand. I thought I'd post a few pictures, she'd say 'yes' and the two of them would go out on a nice date for Valentine's and find out they really like each other."

"You did this? Does Evan know?"

"Yeah, he knows. He saw one of the posts on the shop computer. He was furious."

"Oh wow, so are you going to stop posting? 'Cause I think that Lucy is kind of curious. She didn't say that she would say yes, but Ashley and I convinced her to buy a really cute dress for Valentine's."

Kyle smiled, "I already stopped. Evan has been giving me the cold shoulder, but a couple of days after he found out what I'd done, he started posting himself."

Now Randi smiled. "Well, who knew that you were such a matchmaker."

"You won't tell, will you?"

"Are you kidding? I love this. Evan and Lucy would be a great match. I wish I'd seen it sooner."

They ran from the Hermosa Pier to the Redondo Pier and headed back, nodding to friends and fellow beach goers. They'd hit an easy, compatible stride. The cool January air washed over Randi and her brain churned with ideas to help facilitate the romance.

"Thanks for the run," Randi said.

"Thanks for not telling Lucy that you recognized Evan," Kyle responded.

"No problem, I think they're a great match, and even if Evan's mad at you right now, you're a good brother for trying."

They slowed a little more as they turned onto Pier Avenue. Kyle headed to the Beach Break Coffee Bar, and Randi headed up to her old apartment over Randi's Rags. She hadn't lived in the apartment since marrying Colin, but it was convenient for showering after a run, and taking lunch breaks. Also, it was a great place to hide Christmas gifts!

# Chapter 9

"Seriously, Luce, this guy is great! You need to respond," Ashley said between bites of her chicken salad sandwich.

"It's going to be too late if you don't respond soon," Brenda Chu, one of the third-grade teachers said as she sat next to Ashley in the teachers' lounge.

"But *I don't know who he is*!" Lucy responded to both, putting her yogurt cup down on the table with a smack heavier than she'd intended. "Sorry."

"Seriously, he's got other girls coming on to him. This last picture of the rescue dog booth at the Hermosa Street Fair last summer has all of the girls interested. @beachbabe310 said *maybe @LucySchoolmarm isn't the one for you, @TheGuy4U!*" Ashley read.

"And @sbdoglover posted *@TheGuy4U, I'd rescue dogs with you any day*," Brenda added.

Juan dropped his lunch in front of the seat next to Lucy. "I've got your back, Luce. I'm going to start stalking some of the cute girls who want TheGuy4You.

I've got my eye on @stargazer. She's got some bikini pics
that—"

"Shut up, Juan," Ashley said rolling her eyes. "This
isn't about your depraved love life; this is about Lucy.
Help or go back to your classroom."

"Okay, Lucy. You need to get in the game, start asking
him some questions." Juan turned the paper bag holding
his lunch upside down, and opened a bag of chips. "Ask
him what kind of dog he has, what kind of music he
plays, what his favorite books are…"

"Yeah," Brenda broke in. "Ask him who his favorite
author is. Does he prefer sunrise or sunset? what is his
favorite color?"

"But I don't want to lead him on—"

"Ba-lo-ney," Ashley drew the word out. "You're just
chicken. We're tired of seeing you mope around here.
Cory is gone. He was a nice guy, then he was a crap head.
There are no guarantees, except, that if you don't start
dating again, you'll be alone…that's guaranteed."

Everyone got very quiet, and Lucy looked down at her
yogurt container.

"Ashley!" Brenda broke the silence.

"Ash, that was kind of harsh," Juan said.

"No, no she's right." Lucy picked up her phone from
the table, and began typing.

"What are you doing?" Ashley asked in a panicked
voice, as all of them at the table retrieved their phones

waiting to see.

"You'll see."

Minutes passed as they all waited, then…ping…ping…ping. All of the phones started pinging notifications.

\*\*\*

"@TheGuy4U. *Do you ride your skateboard to work? What kind of music do you play? How did you serve the halibut? What books would be in your basket? And did you take a dog home from the rescue? #stillnotsure #valentinesiscoming #waitingtolearnmore @LucySchoolmarm.*" She'd posted a picture of Roscoe, the big Saint Bernard that lived at The Either Or Bookstore, sitting in a big overstuffed chair next to a pile of books. Evan smiled as he looked at the screen. She'd finally responded. Now how to respond back. He didn't want to lose her interest.

"Hey, dude, she po—"

"I know, dude." Evan smiled without looking at Kyle, who had leaned down and put his elbows on the desk so he could see the computer screen.

"What are you going to do? You've got to be careful if you don't want to give it away too soon."

"I know, I'm freaking out." But Evan's grin was big and easy.

"Still mad at me?"

Evan looked up at Kyle from the chair he was sitting in and slugged his brother in the shoulder. "I haven't decided yet, dude, it depends on what happens. You better hope this doesn't go bad."

Kyle grinned. He hadn't seen Evan smile about a girl in a long time. "It won't. I think she likes you."

"Well, she likes TheGuy4U. We'll have to wait and see if she likes me."

"So, what are you going to say? She asked you a lot of questions."

Evan clicked the page off the screen. "Don't know yet, I'm going to think about it." He got up from the chair and floated out of the room.

Kyle took over the chair his brother had vacated, clicked the screen back on, and put his feet up on the table, crossing his arms and smiling.

# Chapter 10

Lucy was curled up in the flannel pajamas her mother had given her for Christmas. They were printed with books and coffee mugs, the perfect jammies for spending a cozy Friday night reading her historical romance novel. This was the longest it had ever taken her to read a book. Normally she could read a book in a day or two max, but it suddenly felt as though her life had become a romance novel, with secret admirers and friends plotting to put them together.

She tried to pick up with Lady Everly in a carriage on her way to a party at…no, she didn't remember that passage, she'd have to go back, she flipped through the pages trying to find a passage she remembered, but she'd been reading a page here and a page there, and suddenly she was lost and needed to start over. Forget it, she didn't feel like reading anyway.

She turned on the television, and flipped the channels looking for a good movie, maybe an old black and white, or something fun from the eighties. But nothing caught her attention. She tapped her foot on the bottom of the coffee table, then picked up her tablet. Nothing new on her social media, and tossed it beside her. Reluctantly she admitted the source of her restlessness. When would TheGuy4U respond to her questions?

She grabbed her phone and sent a text to Ashley. *Are you busy? Do you want to go to a movie?*

She turned the television back on and stopped on a rerun of Three's Company. Her phone buzzed. *Sorry, Trevor and I are having dinner with his parents. Why don't you see if Randi is available?*

Lucy texted back, *that's okay, I think I'll just have a pizza delivered and read my book. Have fun.*

She got up, and headed toward the kitchen, she should just make some dinner. But there was nothing in the pantry except a box of mac and cheese, a jar of peanut butter, and a couple of cake mixes. The refrigerator wasn't much better. There were three eggs, and a carton of expired cottage cheese. Maybe she *would* order pizza. As she shut the refrigerator door, she saw the flier from the Coffee Bar hanging on the front with a magnet. BATTLE OF THE BANDS FRIDAY, JANUARY 19.

The Coffee Bar. That would get her out of the house and distract her from TheGuy4U.

# Chapter 11

The Beach Break Coffee Bar was packed. She got in line at the counter hoping she'd be able to find a seat.

"Hey, Lucy." She scanned the crowded room trying to find the person calling her name. "Lucy, join us over here." It was Mindi one of the girls who worked at Randi's Rags and she was with a guy. Lucy slowly pressed through the mob of people. Somehow they even had a chair for her. They were at the back of the room, which put them right up front near the stage.

"What are you guys doing here?" Lucy asked.

"Several of Dale's customers are in a couple of the bands playing tonight, so we thought we'd come and listen. You know my cousin Dale, right?"

"Of course! Hi Dale, how's your year going so far?" Dale owned a guitar shop just around the corner on Hermosa Avenue. She started to sit, then stopped. He had longish hair...local boy, owns a business, guitars. He'd definitely seen her riding around town on her bike.

Last time she'd seen him, he'd had a girlfriend.

"Hey, Lucy, isn't that the dress you bought at the store last week?" Mindi pointed to a cute little blonde in the black 'Audrey Hepburn' dress she'd bought at Randi's Rags.

"That's the dress." Lucy felt her cheeks heat up.

"Can I take your order?" Thankfully, a server interrupted. Dale already had a beer, and Mindi a glass of wine, so only Lucy needed to order.

"Oh, yes, a glass of Pinot Grigio, and the fruit and cheese platter." Lucy sat down as the waitress left to get her order. The bands weren't scheduled to start for another half hour; the three of them sat and chatted comfortably.

"Where's your girlfriend, Dale? I'm sorry, I don't remember her name."

"Shauna took a job in Texas six months ago. We thought we could do long distance, that lasted about three weeks, then she met some cowboy."

"Yep, Dale is single...no girlfriend...all alone," Mindi said all too innocently.

"Shut up, Mindi," Dale said, but he smiled as he said it. "Yeah, just me and my skateboard, hanging around town."

"You ride a skateboard? I don't have enough coordination, I'm better on my bicycle!" Lucy checked 'rides a skateboard' off on her mental tally.

"You could learn if you wanted to, but you look cute riding around town on your bike."

Lucy realized they were leaving Mindi out of the conversation. "Mindi, you ride a skateboard, don't you?"

"All over. I'm a beach girl to the bone. I'm going to check in with Randi, she said that she might come over after the shop closed, and that's in five minutes." She was already tapping away.

"So Lucy, don't you work at Beachside Elementary School?"

"I do, I teach fourth grade."

"That's a great age. Perfect age for them to start music lessons. We teach kids from ages seven up at the shop, but I think about nine or ten is really a good age for them to start. What made you pick fourth grade?"

"I taught second grade for one year, and I student taught in a first-grade class, then they lost two fourth grade teachers and bumped me up. I can't say I really picked fourth grade, but I love teaching them. The little ones are fun, but by fourth grade, they're starting to have their own ideas, they can read and discuss books and social studies, and they're still pretty sweet."

"I can see that. I've got this little girl, Tasha, she's been playing for about two years now. She's getting into the history of rock right now, and she wants to talk about the musicians, and what made Jimmy Hendrix write that kind of music? Why isn't there music like that anymore?"

"Tasha Pierce? She was in my class last year. Smart girl!"

"Hey guys," Mindi interrupted. "Randi and Colin aren't going to make it. I have the beginnings of a migraine headache. Would you guys mind if I slip out before the bands start?"

As if on cue, one of the band members got in front of the mic "Sound check. One, two."

Mindi winced a little too dramatically, but Dale didn't seem to notice. "No Cuz, go ahead. Lucy and I'll be fine."

Lucy smiled. "Of course, take care of yourself, Mindi."

Mindi had barely left before someone took her chair.

"I see you around town on your bicycle. Do you have a car?" Dale asked.

"No, I get around pretty well on public transportation if I need to leave the South Bay, but most of my life is right here. There's so much to do here, and my family lives just down the way. I chose to have the beach apartment over a car. Even though I'm getting a good deal on it, the rent is outrageous, so it was eat, or buy a car...I went with eat...oh, and I have to have my books. Do you read?"

"Are you ready to hear some great music?" Kyle's voice interrupted the conversation as he got the crowd's attention. "I said...ARE YOU READY TO HEAR SOME GREAT MUSIC?"

This time the crowd responded with a resounding "YES".

"All of our bands tonight are local bands, we auditioned more than thirty of the best in the South Bay, and it wasn't easy to decide which to bring on stage tonight, they were all so good! We believe we are bringing you the best of the best. Our first group plays what they call punk folk fusion. We just call it good music. Please welcome 'The Can't Make it to Breakfast Club'."

The packed room erupted in applause as the band began to play.

***

Kyle had been watching Lucy's table all night. He was a little worried. He'd overheard part of the conversation, and it sounded as though Lucy thought Dale was TheGuy4U. Evan needed to make this happen, there were only three more weeks until Valentine's. He knew Dale, and had a hard time believing that he would move in and take advantage of the situation. He'd never seemed like an opportunist, but that's exactly what it looked like he was doing. Of course, he didn't know that Evan was The Guy4U.

'The Can't Make it to Breakfast Club' played five songs, then there was an intermission as they broke down their equipment, and the next band set up.

Kyle made his way to Lucy's table. "Hi Lucy, Dale." He tried not to show the animosity that he was feeling. "Are you having fun?"

"Yes!" Lucy answered with a quick smile. "This is great, Kyle."

"Nice line up, Kyle. I have students in two of the upcoming bands."

"Is that so, Dale? Can I get you guys a couple of fresh drinks? Pinot Grigio for you, Lucy, and what about you, Dale?"

"Red Tide," Dale answered, referring to the local IPA microbrew. "Put them both on my tab."

"Oh no!" Lucy said. "I'll pay for mine." She turned to Dale. "You don't need to do that."

"I insist. Kyle, please put the drinks on my tab."

Kyle looked from Lucy to Dale. He wasn't happy with this development. "Anything you say." He nodded and went to get the drinks.

Behind the counter, Evan poured drinks and distributed them to the waiters and waitresses they'd hired for the evening.

"Dude, I think you may need to bump up your plan a little. Looks like Dale's moving in on your girl."

"What?"

"Lucy— I think she thinks Dale's you, or at least she thinks he's TheGuy4U."

Evan looked up as he opened a couple of bottles of

beer. "No way. Dale isn't even her type."

"Well, right now, he's looking like her type. Step it up here."

Kyle handed the drink order to a waitress and headed toward the stage to announce the next band.

Kyle kept an eye on Lucy and Dale as he stepped onto the stage. "Our next band is a punk band that can be seen in their pastel wetsuits, with their pastel hair, surfing right here by the Hermosa Pier. Don't let all of that purple distract you, these ladies know how to make music. Please welcome the Unicorns."

Five girls with varying shades of sherbet colored hair began to play. As he left the stage Kyle noticed that Evan had decided to serve Lucy and Dale's order himself. Good boy. He looked around the Coffee Bar, things were running smoothly, he decided he could disappear for a few minutes.

# Chapter 12

"Excuse me for a few minutes. I need to use the ladies room," Lucy said.

"Of course," Dale said, standing to help her with her chair. And he's a gentleman. She thought, as she pushed her way through the crowd toward the back hallway.

There were so many people here tonight. She stood in a long line that spilled into the hallway and waited for one of the two stalls.

"Hey, aren't you @LucySchoolmarm? You look just like your picture." A girl ahead of her in line called out. Her friend poked her head around and squealed with delight.

"It's really you! LucySchoolmarm!" Seriously? Lucy's jaw dropped. Are that many people paying attention to an online romance, er…situation?

"Hey!" another girl behind her shouted. I thought you looked familiar. That guy you're sitting with, is he TheGuy4U?"

"I-uh, I don't know. I'm not sure who it is yet!"

"So you're cheating on TheGuy4U?" Another girl asked, her tone bordering on angry.

"No, I uh…"

"You know, he's a great guy, I can tell. You really shouldn't be treating him this way."

Lucy's eyes widened in surprise at the heat of this stranger's words. She turned to leave, but realized the hallway was packed and she was surrounded by curious, even angry women. She didn't have an escape.

She started to panic, but suddenly Evan appeared out of nowhere, and pushed people aside to make a narrow aisle leading her out the back door. "This has gotten crazy," she whispered desperately. She felt a little sick. Her hands trembled. "I can see that," Evan said evenly, holding her steady. "Are you okay?"

"Yeah, I think so."

"So are you and Dale a thing?"

"No, I mean, I don't…well, we just ran into each other by accident. He was here with Mindi, but she had to…" he was looking deeply into her eyes and she found it very disconcerting, "I mean…"

Evan leaned down as though he was going to kiss her, his steel grey eyes piercing into her soul, her heart pounded manically, and she could feel goosebumps on her neck and arms, then he stopped. There was a question in his eyes, but he didn't ask it. "You probably should go before someone follows us. I'll make sure Dale knows you had to leave."

"Oh, but my tab!"

"Don't worry about it, this is my fault anyway. I'll take care of it."

"Thanks, Evan, I appreciate it."

*** 

The throng of people in the back hallway had diminished a little, but the place was even more crowded as Evan made his way back into the Coffee Bar. He held back a smile as he found Dale still alone listening to the Unicorns and tapping his foot to the beat. A girl in a #PleaseSayYes tee shirt had scooted her chair closer to Dale's but he didn't seem to notice. As the Unicorns finished the last song in their set, Evan leaned over and whispered to Dale. "Hey Dude, Lucy asked me to tell you she had to leave."

"Really, did she say why? I thought we were having fun."

"Sorry man, she didn't say."

"That's weird."

"Eh women, right?"

Evan kept an eye on Dale the rest of the night. He was never alone. A couple of girls that he'd never seen before joined Dale at the little table, and eventually a couple of people from one of the band's. Dale danced, talked, flirted. He didn't seem too invested in a relationship with Lucy. That was just the way Evan wanted it.

# Chapter 13

On Sunday, as Lucy walked down to the Beach Break Coffee Bar to meet Ashley she found herself going over Friday night in her head. Dale was very charming, and he could be TheGuy4U. He owned his own business, played guitar, had a skateboard. He also had shown a lot of interest in her.

Then there was Evan, quiet, steady Evan. There was no way he was TheGuy4U, but the way he'd looked at her in the alley. She'd thought he was going to kiss her, or maybe she'd just wanted him to kiss her. The situation had been so romantic; he'd ridden in like a knight in shining armor and rescued her from the throng of crazy women in the hallway. Okay, that might be a little dramatic, but he had helped her escape. And he'd said something a little strange. He'd said, "this is my fault anyway". What could he have meant by that? The throng of girls waiting for her couldn't possibly be his fault, all of the people following the Framed posts…no, he must have felt responsible because it was his coffee bar. Wait, it was HIS coffee bar.

"You're @LucySchoolmarm aren't you?" Lucy's thoughts were interrupted by a young girl walking up The Strand with her friend.

"Yes," Lucy responded. Both girls wore red tee shirts with big white hearts on them. The shirts said #PleaseSayYes in the middle of the heart in bold black letters. Lucy was shocked.

"You are going to say 'yes' aren't you?" the first girl asked.

"It's so romantic! I'd love for a guy to pursue me like that," the second girl gushed.

"Where did you get those shirts?" Lucy asked confused.

"Oh, at the guitar shop around the corner. They have them at Randi's Rags too."

"You're kidding," she said stunned. She turned taking a few steps toward Pier Ave.

"Wait, will you autograph our shirts?" the first girl asked. Lucy turned around in astonishment. The girl was holding a fine point marker in her hand.

Sigh, she might as well give them what they wanted. She signed each of their shirts @LucySchoolmarm.

"We follow you on *Framed*. I'm @JennaBakes and she's @MakeupMaven."

"Well, say 'hi' to me when you're online." Lucy said awkwardly. Last night a girl was wearing her dress, not a big deal because the shop was just down Pier Avenue from the Coffee Bar. But now tee shirts? She was going to have a talk with both Randi and Dale. What kind of guy would try to capitalize on a potential relationship? Was that the kind of guy she wanted to be around, and Randi was her oldest friend! What the heck?

She headed up Pier Avenue, and directly to Randi's Rags. As she walked in the door the first thing to catch her eye was the display of tee shirts and tote bags, all saying #PleaseSayYes. Her feet froze in place and her jaw dropped. Really?

"What do you think?" Randi's voice startled her. "They've been selling like crazy! Everyone in town is excited about your Valentine's date with @TheGuy4U. They're selling in our online boutique too. You've gone viral. You are going to say 'yes' aren't you? I have a batch made up that say #SheSaidYes for Valentine's Day."

"Randi, how could you do this? You're capitalizing on my real personal life!"

"When opportunity knocks! Anyway, it wasn't my idea. It was Ashley's, and I thought it was a great one. And read the sign, I'm not keeping the profit. It's all going to Beachside Elementary School's new library. Your cause. I was pretty sure you'd be happy to get the support. Oh, and Jan at the souvenir shop is carrying them, and Dale at the guitar store. You'll have a new library for your kids in no time."

Lucy let out a long breath. How could she be mad? They were all contributing to the renovation of the school library, her pet project.

"Here, you should have a set." Randi handed her a shirt and a bag.

"I can't walk around town with these!"

"Take them as a keepsake. Who knows when something so amazing will ever happen again!"

Lucy closed her mouth and accepted the tote bag and tee shirt, which she rolled up and slipped into her bag. "Randi, what do you know about D—"

"Oh, hi Lucy," Mindi called as she walked in from the back-stock room. "Are you okay? Dale said you left abruptly Friday night. He was worried he'd offended you."

"No, I'm so sorry but the weirdest thing happened. I went to the restroom, and was practically accosted by a group of women who wanted to know if Dale was TheGuy4U, or if I was cheating on TheGuy4U. They were really angry, it was scary. I had a great time with Dale, I asked Evan to let him know what happened." She'd have to get Randi's opinion of Dale another time. "How's your head?"

"What?" Mindi asked. "Oh, much better thank you. I went home and went straight to bed. Sleep in a dark, quiet room, that always helps."

"Glad you're feeling better. Well, I guess I'll talk to you guys later. Have to get my cup of coffee."

"What were you going to ask me, Lucy?"

"Oh, I don't remember, must not have been important." Lucy left the store feeling a little shell-shocked.

# Chapter 14

Randi and Mindi held in their squeals until they were sure Lucy was out of earshot.

"Do you think we did the right thing? That's kind of scary, those girls giving Lucy a bad time," Mindi said.

"I'm sure it was a fluke. Friday couldn't have gone better. Lucy seems a little unnerved by all that's happened. I'm pretty sure she thinks Dale is @TheGuy4U. Kyle called yesterday asking what the heck was going on, and why your cousin was taking advantage of the situation. He said Evan was furious. I didn't tell him this was our doing. Thanks for the help, Mindi."

"Dale was happy to go along with the idea and give Evan a little push. It couldn't have happened more perfectly. He'd just agreed to help me, and we were trying to figure out how to set the whole thing up when Lucy walked into the Beach Break."

"It seems like the whole world wants this to happen.

You should call Dale and tell him Lucy's getting her morning coffee."

Mindi reached into her pocket and pulled out her cell phone.

***

"Here's your hazelnut latte," Evan said, placing a steaming cup and a plate with a muffin in front of Lucy. "What are you reading?"

Lucy looked up from her romance novel and blushed. "Oh, it's—"

"Lucy! What great timing," Dale interrupted as he walked into the coffee bar and made a beeline straight to Lucy, pulling out his wallet and removing some bills as he walked. "Could you bring me a double Americano, and one of those amazing blueberry muffins you've got?" he said to Evan as he pulled out a chair. Evan walked away, grumbling something incoherent as he left. "Do you mind if I join you?"

Lucy smiled, he was already sitting down and he *was* pretty cute. She dropped her book into her purse. "Not at all, I'd enjoy the company."

***

Evan could practically feel the steam coming out of his

ears. He thought Dale was a better friend than this. How could he horn in on Evan's girl? Hmmm, to be fair, she wasn't his girl…yet, and Dale didn't know that Evan was TheGuy4U. He was however, taking advantage of a situation set up by someone else. Evan decided it was time to act. He needed to post another picture. It had to be done just right, enough to knock Dale out of the running, but not enough to give away that Evan was TheGuy4U. There were less than three weeks until Valentine's, he needed to get her to respond. It was getting to be time to ask for that date.

He screwed up several orders paying more attention to Lucy and Dale at the table near the window than to his other customers. When Kyle came in at one o'clock, Lucy and Dale were long gone. But, they'd left together, and Evan was still agitated. He took off his apron, slamming it on the counter. "I'm leaving. I have something to do."

"Hey, wait, I have some marketing stuff to take care of in the office," Kyle said as Evan hopped over the counter and headed to the door.

"Tina will be in at three. It can wait until then." And Evan was out the door.

It was dark by the time Evan returned. Tina was at the counter taking orders, and Kyle was in the back office working on the computer. A man with a mission, Evan started up the stairs.

The building was three stories tall. The first floor was

of course the Coffee Bar, it's office and a small stockroom. The second and third floors were their apartment, with the living room and kitchen on the second floor and the bedrooms on the third floor. There was one last flight of stairs that led to their rooftop patio with an amazing view of the Pacific Ocean. Several of the older buildings were set up this way. Stopping on the first floor of their apartment, Evan rummaged around the cabinets filling some bags and a cardboard box with various items. He gathered his bags and the box and headed up the next flight of stairs. When he got to the rooftop patio he set everything down and went to work.

The round patio table had to be moved. He dragged it to the southwest corner of the rooftop. He didn't want any signs or landmarks to show up in the picture and give away the location, but he wanted to show that it was a rooftop patio, and Dale didn't have a rooftop patio. Dale lived in a little bungalow on the other side of Hermosa Avenue. Dale would be out of the running without giving away Evan's identity.

He pulled out the white tablecloth he'd purchased, shook it out and spread it over the table. He should probably iron it. Hopefully the folds wouldn't show up in the picture. He added a vase with red silk roses, and spread some silk rose petals around the vase. Next, he put a couple of crystal candleholders on the table and placed a red tapered candle in each holder. He set two white plates on the table and neatly folded two red napkins, placing them on the plates. He placed a wine glass at each place setting and put a bottle of Pinot Grigio, Lucy's favorite wine, on the table. He stood back to admire his handiwork. Not bad for a guy. He flipped the switch by the door, and white lights twinkled all around the rooftop. All that was left was to light the candles and take some pictures.

# Chapter 15

"What the heck is going on outside? Is it a high-speed pursuit?" Randi asked as she unlocked the shop door, let herself in, then turned to lock it again. It was nine-thirty on Monday morning. Outside a news helicopter flew overhead, and several drones were crisscrossing the promenade. The noise was deafening.

"I don't know. I turned the television on, but I can't find any news," Mindi responded from behind the counter where she was putting tags on some new stock.

It was a little quieter inside the store. Randi peeked out the window watching the scene outside. There was a small crowd forming on the promenade. "Hey, I think that's Christina Pascucci out there. Turn on Channel Five."

"Sure boss." Mindi headed to the back room to turn on the television, as Randi took one more peek out the front window then headed to join her.

***

Down at the Coffee Bar, Kyle and Evan already had their television set to Channel Five, and all eyes in the coffee bar were glued to Christina.

"We're on Pier Avenue in Hermosa Beach. As you can see there are drones and even a news helicopter flying overhead. I hope you can hear me over the noise. So, what's this all about? Is there a surf competition? Kite festival?" A drone whizzed right over Christina's head. "A drone show? No, this is all about a viral online romance that has captured the hearts of South Bay residents, all of Los Angeles and even the rest of the country. A Framed poster, with the anonymous profile TheGuy4U, has been posting photos on Framed tagging another poster, LucySchoolmarm, a local school teacher, as he woos her, hoping for a Valentine's Date."

***

Up the street at Beachside Elementary the kids were on their first recess and Lucy walked into the teachers' lounge. Six teachers were sitting at the lunch table eyes glued to the television, three were wearing #PleaseSayYes tee shirts.

"Are you kidding me?"

"Shush, you need to watch this." Ashley pointed at the screen.

There was a screenshot of the most recent post TheGuy4U had made early this morning. A table set on a rooftop at night with little white lights hanging from the railing, the black ocean waters visible in the background, under the moonlight. It was hard to make out anything else in the background in the darkness of the night.

"Seriously, this is on the news?"

"Shush," the row of teachers said, but the story had ended and they shut off the television.

"What was that all about? And do you guys really have to wear those shirts?"

"You've gone viral, Lucy, truly viral. Everyone is down in Hermosa trying to figure out which rooftop that picture was taken from. They figure because of the height it was shot from and the distance from the beach it has to be one of the buildings on Pier Avenue or possibly Hermosa Avenue. People are out there with drones, trying to look on rooftops for anything that matches the picture." Melissa said. The small group of teachers started talking all at once.

"You need to respond, Lucy. He asked for the date, you have to give him an answer."

"It's time. You need to say yes."

"Are you going to wear the black dress? I have a hat you can borrow."

"You're a celebrity, everyone will be following you two on this date."

Lucy turned and walked back out the door.

***

"Inside voices people," Ashley said. "Look what you did, you scared her off. Now I have to go talk her off the ledge." But the bell rang, signaling the end of recess, and the teachers all returned to their classrooms. Ashley ducked her head into Lucy's classroom as she walked by. "I'll see you for dinner tonight." She left before Lucy could respond.

***

Ashley met Lucy at her classroom. "You can't take your bike. News people are waiting in front of the school to talk to you."

"What am I going to do? How do I get out of here?"

"Don't worry, just grab your stuff, I have a plan." Ashley led Lucy to Gunther, the custodian's room. Just outside his door was a large box and the small Cushman vehicle that he used for hauling things around campus, also known as the Gunther-Mobile. It was kind of like a golf cart with a flatbed on the back. "Hop on the back."

"What?" Lucy asked.

"Hop on, we're going to get you out of here."

Lucy sat down on the back of the truck bed, and Gunther helped Ashley pick up the box which had the bottom cut out and put it over Lucy.

"What the heck? I have to leave like this?" Lucy's voice came muffled through the box.

"Or, you could say *thank you*," Ashley said, then hopped into the front with Gunther, and they sped away. They reached the service parking and came to a stop. Ashley and Gunther both looked around cautiously. No one was there. The media and curious onlookers were all near the teachers' parking where Lucy's bike was chained up, and at the front of the school. Ashley and Gunther lifted the box, and rushed Lucy into the open door of a waiting school minivan with tinted back windows.

"Thanks, Gunther," Ashley said as she hopped into the driver's seat, then, "Stay down in back, so they don't see you."

Lucy curled up on the seat and hid under her jacket as Ashley carefully pulled away through the service driveway. She drove the few blocks to Lucy's apartment, but as she looked down the alley she could see that there were people all around the building. She just kept driving.

"Where are we going?" Lucy asked from the backseat.

"Just be quiet and stay down. We can't go to your apartment. We have to get out of here."

Finally, Ashley pulled the vehicle to a stop and said, "Okay, this is it for now. I can't take the van any farther. We'll have Juan come and pick it up. Melissa is bringing my car over."

Lucy got out of the vehicle slightly disoriented by having ridden curled up on her side.

"Where are we? This isn't your place."

"Are you sure?"

"Ash, I'm not in the mood."

"This is Trevor's place. I have a key. I'll call him and let him know we're here, but we couldn't go to your place, the street was crawling with people, and my place is too close to all of the chaos. Everyone is looking for you. I'm sure they want to know what you're going to say and if you know who it is. Do you…know who it is?"

Ashley jiggled the key in the lock and finally got the door open. She closed the door behind them, and they both stood in the entryway of Trevor's little Redondo Beach house for a few moments of stunned silence.

"Come in, let's catch our breath." Ashley ushered Lucy to the sofa, taking her jacket and bag and tossing them onto a recliner. The room was small and Trevor had oversized, comfy furniture filling the space.

Lucy sat down and sighed.

"Okay," Ashley said. "Do you have any idea who it is?"

"I thought it was Dale, Mindi's cousin, but now I

don't think so. He told me he had one of the little cottages one block up the hill from Hermosa Avenue. He doesn't have a rooftop patio, or even an ocean view. I guess he could have used someone else's roof."

"I don't think so," Ashley was strolling through Framed on her phone looking for the post. "His post says...*if you say yes, dinner for two on my rooftop patio, Valentine's night, weather permitting.*"

"Yeah, he probably wouldn't have said *my* rooftop patio if he was using someone else's."

Ashley continued to read on her cell phone. "Everyone is trying to figure out which rooftop it is, but they're having a hard time. They're looking everywhere along the coast, Manhattan Beach, Hermosa and Redondo. They think by the picture it has to be one of the buildings on Hermosa Avenue, possibly one of the smaller walk streets down to the beach. In other words, they just know it's got an ocean view."

Chuck Berry's song from the fifties, 'School Days,' began playing in Lucy's bag. She searched in her purse and retrieved her cell phone. "It's Karrie," she said to Ashley. Karrie Emerson was the school principal. She pushed the button to pick up the phone, bracing herself for the worst. "Hello?"

"Hi Lucy, this is Karrie. I think we need to talk about the current situation."

"I'm so sorry, Mrs. Emerson." Lucy felt like a student

in trouble and reverted to the principal's last name. "I have no control over what's going on. I'm not sure how to make it stop."

"I'm not upset with you. I've been watching the whole thing, and I think it's kind of sweet. I even have my own #PleaseSayYes tote bag. However, we do have to consider the children, and after the chaos that happened today, I've gotten a substitute to teach your class— and I think you should take some sick days. I'm sure after Valentine's Day this will all go away. Do you have enough sick days or personal days left?"

"Thank you. Yes, I haven't taken any days this year, so I have plenty of time. I'm so sorry. I'm trying to figure out how to get to my apartment. My lesson plans are posted on my school page." Valentine's was next Wednesday, so if she had to take both this week and next week off she'd deplete most of her sick days. She'd better stay healthy the rest of the year.

"That's fine. Maybe you can post some kind of message to your students each day. They all seem to be following your Framed romance. Something appropriate that lets them feel part of it. And I'll check in with you at the end of the week."

"I can do that. Thank you, Mrs. Emerson."

"You're not in trouble, I'm still Karrie…oh and I vote that you say yes! Talk to you soon." And with that the line disconnected.

"So what did she say? Was she ticked off about all of the news people there?"

"She was very understanding, told me to take some time off, and that she thinks I should say 'yes'." Lucy was mortified; she couldn't believe her principal was following this whole thing.

"So, what *are* you going to say and how are you going to say it? Valentine's is next week, and he's probably expecting an answer. It has to be pretty special, I mean, you are saying 'yes' right?"

"I don't know what to do. I'm back to square one. I know it's not Dale, and I don't have a clue who it is." She saw Evan's face Sunday night after he helped her escape, he'd looked almost angry that she'd been with Dale, and then she'd thought he was going to kiss her. If Evan asked her out she'd say yes, but Evan wouldn't do this. She'd been having coffee in his shop since they opened three years ago, and they'd only had a handful of conversations. Never small talk, he didn't do that, they were real conversations, but they were rare. Why couldn't a guy like Evan ask her out?

"We can make it safe. Tell him yes, but you can't meet on his rooftop it has to be somewhere public."

"Clearly we can't meet on his rooftop OR somewhere public, everyone will be looking for us!"

"Okay, let me think about this. We can figure this out."

This time Ashley's phone went off, "Hi Randi," she said into the receiver. "Yeah, it's crazy. She's here with me, we're at Trevor's place. We couldn't go back to hers and mine wasn't much better. Really? That would be great. Are you sure we'll be able to get her in there? Okay, call me when you think it's safe." Ashley tapped her phone and set it on the end table.

"Randi says you can stay in the apartment over Randi's Rags, no one's using it right now. She ran past your place this afternoon and said it's swarming with people waiting for you to come home, and it doesn't look like they plan on leaving anytime soon. She thinks if you wait until after all of the stores on Pier Avenue are closed people should be going home. She's going to hang out at the store and give us a call when things die down."

"I don't have anything with me except what's in my computer case, no clothes, toothbrush…and what about food?" Lucy's voice came out high and fast, she wasn't going to be able to go to her own apartment, and she couldn't go to work.

"Stop picking at your nail polish. Look you'll be living over a fashion boutique, I'm sure we can get clothing up to you and I'll pick up some personal items. It'll be easier for us to take food to you and visit you if you're over the shop, no one will be looking for you there."

Lucy let out a long sigh.

They talked for hours. Melissa came by with her

husband and dropped off Ashley's car. Juan picked up the van. They talked some more. Trevor came home from work to find the two girls on his sofa. He ordered pizza, tried to join the conversation, but eventually went to bed and left them alone.

Finally, about ten-thirty Randi called Ashley. "Okay, thanks, we're on our way," Ashley said into the phone.

"Let's steal some food from Trevor's kitchen so you have something there until we can bring you groceries." They threw the leftover pizza, a couple of bananas, some cheese and crackers into a bag and headed out to the car.

# Chapter 16

They drove past Lucy's street on the way to Randi's Rags.
"Oh my gosh, there are still people out there and drones
flying around. I feel so bad for my neighbors. But as they
pulled into the alley behind the little dress shop, the coast
was clear, no news vans or drones, just a couple of people
smoking outside behind the nightclub that was two doors
west of Randi's Rags. Lucy pulled the hood of her
sweatshirt up grabbed her computer bag and the
groceries, and raced toward the back door of Randi's
shop.

*Bzzzz, Bzzzz,* it sounded like a weed whacker as it
came around the corner. Both girls held their bags as they
raced for the back door followed by the drone.

Randi opened the door quickly leading them into the
narrow hallway of the old building, and up a flight of
stairs to a tiny apartment. Inside, they dropped the few
bags onto a little kitchen counter.

"I don't know how to thank you Randi! People are still

outside my apartment building. I can't believe this is happening."

"I'm happy to help you. Mindi knows you're up here, but none of my other employees know anything. If you need something just call or text Mindi or me, and we'll make sure you get it. Make yourself at home. I have some spare clothes in here," Randi led the girls into the small bedroom. "Mostly yoga pants and shirts for running in, but feel free to use them. There are fresh towels in here." She continued the tour, leading the girls into a small bathroom. "And use the shampoo and conditioner, there's more in here." She opened a little cabinet. "Soap too. Use whatever you need." Randi returned through the bedroom to the small living room kitchen area. "There's not much in the kitchen, some tea and I keep a few meals in the freezer, help yourself if you're hungry. And I do have a washer and dryer in this little closet." She opened a door next to the pantry and revealed a stacked apartment size set. "Television in the living room, and the Wi-Fi code is taped to the remote if you have your laptop with you. Relax, we'll check on you tomorrow."

"Thank you. I appreciate this."

"What are friends for, if not hiding you from the paparazzi and news helicopters when you become a social media sensation?" Randi said smiling. "I'll see you tomorrow," she said again, slipping out the front door.

Ashley lingered at the door for a moment.

"I'll come by after work tomorrow. We still have to work out a plan. Text me a list of things you need."

"Thanks, Ashley. Drive carefully," Lucy said.

Ashley reached out and wrapped her arms around Lucy, squeezing her tightly.

"You have to say 'yes'," she said as Lucy shut the door behind her.

How had things gotten so crazy? A few weeks ago, her life was normal. She picked up her coffee every morning at the Beach Break Coffee Bar, rode her bicycle to school, taught a fourth-grade class with twenty-four students, came home and usually read a book. On the weekends, she was happy to curl up with another book, or go out with girlfriends. Peaceful. Quiet. Anonymous. And she'd been quite content.

Or had she? Something had been missing, magic, passion, love... Since Cory left, all of the magic had gone out of life. She could take care of herself just fine, but she liked having a man in her life.

In Randi's bedroom, she opened a dresser drawer and found a big tee shirt. She undressed, dropping her clothes on the floor and crawled into the bed.

Maybe she'd just read too many books. That magical kind of romance, that head-over-heels love, it was only found in romance novels and movies. It wasn't real. Was it? She drifted off to sleep with images running through her head like a slideshow—drones, rooftop patios, Dale's smile as he joined her for coffee and Evan's face just about to kiss her.

# Chapter 17

Sunlight streamed through the bedroom window, and a helicopter roared overhead waking Lucy on Tuesday morning. It took her a minute to fully awaken and remember that she was in Randi's little apartment. She must have slept very late if the sun was shining so brightly. She looked around until she found the digital clock on the bedside table. Nine-thirty-two a.m. Wow, she hadn't realized how tired she'd been. She hopped out of bed. She should shower before Randi or Mindi came up to check on her.

She had showered and dressed in a cute little yoga outfit that she'd found in Randi's dresser when she heard a knock on the front door.

"Who is it?" she called through the closed door.

"Just me," Randi answered from the other side.

Lucy turned the lock and opened the door so Randi could enter, arms laden with food.

"I have one hazelnut latte and a few muffins. Plus, I grabbed some yogurt, salad fixings and fruit at the grocery store before I came in this morning.

"Thank you for all of your help," Lucy said as she grabbed her purse from the kitchen counter where she'd left it the night before. She pulled out a twenty-dollar bill and handed it to Randi.

"No way, let me do this for you."

"The apartment is more than enough. And, I don't know how many days I'll be here."

"Don't worry about it, you've been great business for the store," Randi said with a mischievous grin. Then more seriously, "The store has been so busy because of this. People come in to buy the #PleaseSayYes tee shirts, and the black dress you bought, and they buy more. The least I can do is give you some coffee and muffins. I'm right downstairs if you need anything."

"Can you make the helicopter and drones go away?"

"It is loud up here, isn't it? My headphones are in the desk drawer if you want to try them."

After Randi left Lucy checked her phone and tablet for messages. She'd turned off the volume on her phone last night because it hadn't stopped buzzing with Framed notifications, and text messages from friends and family asking questions. It was time to face the music.

She had thirty-two text messages and fourteen voice messages on her phone from friends and family. Three from her mother. She was going to have to answer a lot of questions. And on Framed she was tagged by more than twelve hundred people. She scrolled through the comments.

*@LucySchoolmarm-will you be meeting@TheGuy4U for a rooftop rendezvous? —@theladyinred*

*@LucySchoolmarm-say YES already, we're all waiting —@beachbabe*

*@TheGuy4U, @LucySchoolmarm is really nice, I know she'll say yes *waves @LucySchoolmarm—@JennaBakes.* Lucy shook her head, that was one of the girls she'd met on The Strand wearing the #PleaseSayYes tee shirt.

*@TheGuy4U- What kind of cookies do you like? I'll bake them and send them with @LucySchoolmarm. @LucySchoolmarm, this is your mother. Say YES. —@LucySchoolmarmsMom*

NO! Not her mom. She clicked on the profile, there was a picture of her mother with a plate full of cookies, her answer to everything. The profile had only been up since last night, and said, South Bay Native, happily married, mother of LucySchoolmarm and two sons. Loves to bake, powerwalk at the beach and read books…and her mother had over six hundred followers.

Well, she couldn't avoid it any longer, she had to call her mom. She'd obviously heard what was going on from friends or on the news…or both.

She scrolled to the icon with her mom's contact

information and pressed 'send'. The phone rang three times then sent her to voice mail. Phew, she was saved.

"Hi, Mom. I'm sorry I haven't called. I know you've seen the chaos. My principal put me on sick leave, and I'm having to hide out at a friend's place for now, but I'm fine. Please don't worry. And no, I don't know if I'm going to say 'yes'. The guy is a total stranger." She paused for a moment. "Love you. Bye." She said quickly and hung up before she could erase the message.

Eventually, she'd have to talk to her mom. Her parents, Peggy and Ralph Vaughn, had met in high school, gotten married six weeks after graduation and been together ever since. Her mother wanted nothing more than to see her daughter happily married to a great guy, and producing grandchildren so that she had someone to eat all of the cookies she baked. Ever since Cory had left for Australia her mother had tried to set Lucy up with her friend's sons, employees at the aerospace company where Ralph had worked for thirty years, friends of Lucy's older brothers, or cute guys she met when she was out and about. It was embarrassing, but Lucy didn't know how to stop it. Her mother was obviously enjoying this new little episode in Lucy's life.

*** 

She had to distract herself from Framed, TheGuy4U, the

helicopters overhead and anything that had to do with #PleaseSayYes. She decided to work on a special project for her kids using the school website and her classroom page. She retrieved her laptop from her school bag. The minute she turned on the power it started pinging like crazy, so she turned off all social media notifications and set about making a video for her kids.

"Hello class, I'm sure you're having fun with your substitute teacher, but I wanted you to know that I miss you and I'm thinking of you. While I'm gone, I have a special project for you. We'll work on it a little at a time. Tonight's homework is to come up with a social media 'handle' for yourself. A handle is a nickname, something you might call yourself instead of your real name. Many of you know that my handle on Framed is LucySchoolmarm. I know you're not old enough to have your own accounts, but I also know most of you know what Framed is. So, even though at school you call me Ms. Vaughn, if you were to 'Frame' me you would tag me @LucySchoolmarm so that I would see the pictures you might post.

"A handle often tells people a little about you. Maybe you're a dancer, or you love dogs, your name might be @TwinkleToes, or @4leggedfriends. You get the idea. I'd like you to talk to your parents or an older sibling and get some input while you come up with your name, then come back here and post your real name with your handle. For example, I would post my name: Ms. Vaughn/@LucySchoolmarm.

"I'll check back with you tomorrow to see what you've come up with!"

She stopped the video, typed a quick email to Ms. Emerson outlining what she planned to do, and asking if she could have the sub contact Lucy, and attached the video.

# Chapter 18

At Beach Break Coffee Bar, Evan was a mess. "This is your fault, Kyle. You started this." He was in the back-office pacing and ranting.

Kyle looked up from the pile of invoices sitting on the desk. "Look dude, you could have stopped it weeks ago, you decided to go for it, and I think it was the right decision. Neither of us could have expected it to get this out of control."

"I don't know what to do! If she says yes, we can't have our rooftop dinner—there will be media everywhere. If she says no, I don't even want to think about it, talk about public humiliation."

"Do I make another post?" Evan continued. "Do I wait for a response? What the heck? And poor Lucy, I heard she had to hide, she can't go to school, no one is sure where she is right now. At least no one knows who I am, but her profile is public."

"Dude, chill out. Wait a couple of days, this will blow over. Plus I think I have an idea how we can work this out. Hold down the fort, I'll be back." Kyle left through the back door.

Kyle popped his head into the back door at Randi's Rags. "Hey Randi!" he called out. "Are you here?"

Muffled voices could be heard in the storefront, then Randi appeared dressed impeccably as always. "Oh, Kyle, hi, what's up? Well, besides the drones and the occasional helicopter?"

"That's what I want to talk to you about, I need to find out what Lucy's answer is going to be, then I need your help."

# Chapter 19

At eight p.m. on Tuesday night, Kyle, Evan, Randi, her husband Colin, and Ashley gathered in the living room of Randi and Colin's sleek modern Santa Monica penthouse condo. Colin, who only knew what little he'd seen on the news was keeping everyone's wine glasses filled, and had been given the task of ordering food for everyone from the little bistro a few blocks down the road.

"I wish Lucy was here. I feel bad that she's trapped in her apartment." Ashley said, then, "Thank you," as Colin filled her glass of wine. "Couldn't we bring her in on a video chat?"

"No, we don't want her here yet, we want this to play out, and right now she still doesn't know that Evan is TheGuy4U," Randi piped in.

"That's right," Kyle added. "And *you* can't tell her," he directed at Ashley.

"I'm not going to tell her, bean brains. I don't want to ruin the whole thing."

"Make sure you don't."

Ashley glared at Kyle over her wine glass.

"Look, we need to figure out what to do. I feel so bad that Lucy is trapped in her house because everyone knows who she is, while I'm able to just keep living my life," Evan broke in.

"Don't worry, Evan. Once they find out who you are, you'll get your fifteen minutes of fame," Kyle rubbed in.

"Okay, everyone," Randi took control of the group. "We have a lot of work to do. Lucy is trapped in my apartment and can't leave. The media won't go away. We need to make this happen. Ashley, do you know if she's going to say 'yes' What we do depends on her answer."

"She's worried because she doesn't know who it is. I think she wants to go, I know she would go if she knew it was Evan. I told her that we would make a plan so that it would be safe, but every plan I came up with didn't work because I didn't know who TheGuy4U was."

"Well, now you can assure her it's safe, and we can make a real plan."

Colin's phone buzzed. "The food's downstairs, I just buzzed the delivery guy in. Why don't you guys move this to the dining room while I meet him at the door."

Randi picked up her wine glass and headed to the dining table, and her guests followed suit.

"Obviously, I can't do the rooftop dinner that everyone is expecting, we wouldn't have a moment of peace." Evan put his glass down on a placemat, next to a paper plate and flatware and sat down.

"But, everyone is expecting the rooftop, and no matter what you change it to, you won't have any peace," Kyle responded.

Colin entered the room with a large box of food and Randi helped him set it out with serving spoons in the middle of the table. "This is a Greek chicken salad, beef shawarma, hummus, tzatziki, and falafel. Pita bread of course, garlic sauce and tahini sauce." Randi pointed to each of the dishes. "Dig in," she invited her guests.

"You realize," Colin broke in now that he had an idea what was really going on, "just because she doesn't know TheGuy4U is Evan, doesn't mean that the only way you can communicate now is on Framed. You could post what you want people to think is going to happen, and Ashley or Randi can convey an entirely different message to Lucy, without spoiling the 'reveal' if you will."

"Okay, that's a good plan, but what can we do, and how can we make it happen without her being followed."

"I think I have a plan," Colin said, and he began to lay it out for them.

***

Lucy was curled up in her blankets scrolling through the homework she'd assigned the kids. Some of the handles they'd come up with were great. Some showed they may have been spending too much time on Framed.

Brayden, a soccer player picked WickedKicks as his handle, Megan came up with MerMegan. Emily's handle was FutureSchoolMarm—how could Lucy not love that? And Joshua picked TheJoshinator. There were so many great handles on the page. She'd already posted her next assignment on the class webpage. The kids were to take a picture for their profile that represented their online handle. They were not to actually be in the picture. Even though the school website was secure, she didn't want them posting pictures of themselves.

Time to do a little online shopping, but her phone rang. It was Ashley.

"Hello? Tell me what's going on."

"All I can tell you is that you should say yes. I promise you it's safe, and I'm pretty sure you won't be sorry."

"You know who it is? Tell me."

"I can't tell you, but you need to post a picture, and when you say yes, we'll take care of everything else."

"We?"

"That's all I can say. I'm going to hang up now because I have a big mouth and don't want to give anything away. Let me know what you're going to do."

Ashley knows who it is, and thinks she should say yes. She got up and paced Randi's little apartment. It was eleven thirty on Tuesday night. She still had a week until

Valentine's. She peeked through the blinds. There were actually still a few people outside, don't they have lives? The helicopters had finally stopped. All day long people had been outside walking on the promenade and The Strand with signs that said #PleaseSayYes, and drones had been flying around looking for clues to the identity of TheGuy4U and trying to get a glimpse of Lucy so they could bombard her with questions.

She made her decision.

\*\*\*

Ashley picked up her phone to check her Framed updates before she even got out of bed. She crossed her fingers that Lucy didn't chicken out. *Say Yes, Say Yes, Say Yes.* Framed wouldn't load! The Framed website had crashed. She sent a quick text to Lucy.

\*\*\*

At the Coffee Bar, Evan quit even trying to help customers or make drinks and handed things over to the two college students they'd hired to help with busy mornings. He went back to the office where Kyle was on the computer.

"Have you checked again?"

"Framed is still down."

"Are you sure check—"Evan stopped talking and turned the volume up on the small television over the desk.

"The popular website Framed crashed this morning within fifteen minutes of a post by @LucySchoolmarm, the South Bay school teacher who has been the focus of much attention since New Year's Eve when her secret admirer @TheGuy4U began wooing her for a Valentine's date. Followers went crazy this morning posting and sharing posts with their friends, bringing down the website for nearly three hours now. If you're sitting at the edge of your seat wondering how LucySchoolmarm answered the hashtag, please say yes, I'm happy to share this screenshot from one of our viewers." A picture of Lucy wearing the popular black dress, her hair pulled into a long sleek side ponytail that hung over her shoulder appeared and she held up a chalkboard with just one word on it. #YES.

"Evan, she said 'yes,' dude. She said YES!" Kyle jumped out of his seat.

Evan didn't move, but his smile said it all.

*** 

Down the block at Randi's Rags, Mindi was opening a box of tee shirts that said #SheSaidYes. "How'd you know she'd say 'yes'?"

"I didn't, I was hoping. But I couldn't lose, lots of people get engaged on Valentine's. The profits are still going to Beachside Elementary Library."

"The little black dresses came in this morning too. Both the one Lucy bought and the one she didn't buy, but there are only enough for the special orders we took. I called the manufacturer, and he said that he couldn't send any more; they've been selling out in every dress shop that carried them," Mindi informed her boss.

"Wow, who would have thought that LucySchoolmarm would become a trendsetter?" Randi said, happy for her friend and enjoying the excitement.

***

Initially Evan had planned to reveal himself in the final post if Lucy said yes to the date. But that was before things went viral. She had been trapped for days in Randi's apartment over the little beach boutique, and would be until their date. He couldn't be trapped too, so now there was a new plan.

Evan posted a photo of a red heart with the words #SheSaidYes, #CantWait. Written across it. It was two days before Valentine's, and he needed to make one more post.

He posted the same rooftop patio photo that had gone viral, only this time the caption read. *Share our romantic*

*Valentine's evening. Celebrate Valentine's with your significant other or a group of special friends, on a rooftop patio, yours, a friend's, one at hotel, restaurant or bar. If it's too cold where you are, just go up long enough to post a picture and comment #PleaseSayYes2Valentine's. I hope you'll share YOUR Valentine's pics. #PleaseSayYes, #2daystoValentines.*

***

Lucy looked in the mirror, she couldn't believe what they were doing to her! Well, she couldn't be more festive.

*Bzzzz.* She headed to the door, checked the peephole then opened it. Randi and Ashley burst in—Randi in a dress she'd designed herself, an adorable pink dress with black trim, black lace along the neckline, and black petticoats. Ashley wore the sexy little red number she'd purchased downstairs at Randi's shop.

"That's it, I'm not going." Lucy said, as they both made an obvious effort not to laugh. She was wearing red tights, red high heels and a huge red heart costume with a red nylon window she could see through. Across the front of the costume was a wide pink sash with the words *Be My Valentine* printed on it.

"It's the only way we're going to get you out of here without being followed," Randi said. "And that cute little number will get you a lot of attention." This time she didn't even try not to laugh.

"If nothing else, he'll know you're all heart," Ashley added.

Lucy turned her back on her friends and took two steps toward the bedroom before they both ran to block the bedroom door.

"It's only to get you out of here. We'll get you all dolled up before you meet your date. Don't worry, it's going to be great," Randi promised as she guided her carefully out the door and to the stairs, letting Ashley grab Lucy's bags and lock the door behind them.

Lucy was still the only one who didn't know who she was spending Valentine's with.

***

"Are you guys done yet?" she asked as Ashley flipped Lucy's long auburn side ponytail into lush soft waves, and Randi closed the clasp on the pearl necklace she'd brought for Lucy to borrow.

"Stand up and look in the mirror," Ashley ordered.

It was eight forty. She was supposed to meet her date in twenty minutes. She stood up, adjusted the strap on the red heels she was wearing and picked up the red satin evening bag Ashley had brought. She walked over to the full-length mirror.

"Is that me?" She smiled at her reflection. "I feel like Cinderella!"

"One more thing," Randi said as she slipped a black satin evening wrap around Lucy's shoulders.

"You look gorgeous, dahling," Ashley drawled.

"You do, Lucy."

"What if we don't like each other?" Lucy turned away from the mirror, fidgeting with the satin wrap.

"Don't worry, you already do." Randi gave her a hug, careful not to miss up her clothes or hair.

Ashley followed, giving her a gentle hug, then squeezing her and hugging harder. "I love you, girlfriend. Enjoy this," she whispered.

Lucy had tears in her eyes.

"Don't cry! You'll ruin your makeup," her friends squealed in unison.

"Okay, let's go."

***

It was quiet as the girls left the hotel at the Redondo Beach Marina. No one had followed them. They could see helicopters and drones up and down the beach, but they were looking for rooftop patios, and Ashley and Randi weren't leading Lucy to a rooftop patio. They walked her onto the dock, leading her along a row of boats until she saw it. *Z' Good Life.* It was Colin's boat named after his favorite design project. Colin was on board, not surprising since it was his boat, Trevor was there waiting for Ashley, but why was Kyle from the Beach Break Coffee Bar here? Lucy recognized his girlfriend, although she couldn't remember her name. It must be a party, she relaxed—a party would be safe and easy. Colin held out a hand to help her onto the boat, and Kyle handed her a glass of champagne.

Finally, all of her friends were standing on the boat with glasses, and she saw a dark figure coming around the corner. She could only see the silhouette of his frame as a spotlight hit him from behind. He was tall, with longish curly hair...and as he came closer she could see him, handsome in his black suit with a red tie, a boyish and slightly unsure smile on his face. It was Evan.

Lucy felt the heat creep into her cheeks as she remembered the night at that night at the Beach Break wishing he would kiss her, even if people would think she was cheating on TheGuy4U she couldn't go out with him because people would think she was cheating on TheGuy4U. But it was him all along.

He put out his hands for hers and she took them.

"You should have told me," her voice was so quiet only he could hear.

"I wanted to, but..."

They were interrupted by Colin. "Let's drink to Evan and Lucy finding each other through all of the chaos and confusion." They all raised their glasses.

"And the next time you two decide to go on a date,

can you please just pick up the phone and call!" Ashley said with a smile.

Glasses clinked, and everyone drank. There were several "Hear, hears!"

"I think we should leave Lucy and Evan in some long-awaited peace," Colin proclaimed. "Plus, I have to show Randi that I'm as romantic as Evan," he said with a devilish grin.

As their friends started to disembark from the boat, Evan led Lucy into the little stateroom. There was a table set for two with a bottle of champagne on ice, a vase of roses, and rose petals scattered about. Candles were lit, and after Evan helped Lucy into her seat, he turned on the stereo, and soft music floated into the room.

He popped open the champagne and refilled her glass. Just as they were about to toast, Kyle bounded into the room.

"I need a picture to post on Framed."

Lucy looked at Evan.

"Let's give the people what they want." He leaned closer to her and kissed her.

She leaned into him and returned the kiss. By the time they pulled apart, Kyle was gone.

All around the South Bay helicopters and drones were searching rooftops looking for @TheGuy4U and @LucySchoolmarm, but the couple floated on the ocean, just on the fringe of the chaos, where no one expected them to be.

# Chapter 20

*You've been Framed.* Lucy clicked the notification on her phone. It was the photo Kyle had taken of her and Evan as they'd kissed last night. The caption read, *Happy Valentines to all of our followers from @TheGuy4U and @LucySchoolmarm.*

Then she scrolled through all the other posts. #PleaseSayYes followers had posted pictures from rooftops all over the country. There were photos of couples having romantic dinners for two, of families sharing the holiday with their children, and rooftop Valentine's parties. There were photos of rooftop proposals with #PleaseSayYes and #SheSaidYes. There were photos of singles on rooftops holding signs that said #PleaseSayYes.

Lucy was amazed at the number of people who responded. People could have searched all night and never found Evan's rooftop. Not that it would have mattered if they did!

Who would have thought such a crazy thing would happen to little Lucy the school teacher? She clicked back to the post that had started everything—Evan's skateboard in the sand.

Now her school was getting a new library, and she was pretty sure that this incredible guy was her boyfriend.

A text message popped up as she looked through the messages. She clicked on it.

*I'm standing outside with your hazelnut latte and a brownie. Can I come in? #PleaseSayYes.*

**THE END**

# About the Author

Tari Lynn Jewett lives in Southern California with her husband of more than 30 years, Paul, also known as Hunky Hubby. They have three amazing sons, a board game designer, a sound engineer and a musician, all who live nearby. For more than fifteen years she wrote freelance for magazines and newspapers, wrote television commercials, radio spots, numerous press releases, and many, MANY PTA newsletters. As much as she loved writing those things, she always wanted to write fiction…and now she is.

She also believes in happily ever afters…because she's living hers.

Links:

Tari's Website: tarilynnjewett.com
Follow Tari on
Facebook: facebook.com/tarilynnjewett
Twitter: @TariLynnJewett
Instagram: instagram.com/tarilynnjewett

# Coming Soon from Tari Lynn Jewett

## #Haunted Hermosa

## Book Two in the #Hermosa for the Holidays series

Ten years ago, Mindi McConnell had her first big crush, on Adam Kovac. Adam played the drums for The Sound Waves, her cousin, Dale's band. His long, wavy beach hair, and the fact he played in a band made him hard to resist.

But Adam had brushed her off and treated her like a little girl.

Now Adam's back in Hermosa Beach, and Mindi just wants him to leave her alone. But Hermosa is a small town and it's impossible to avoid him. Did he really have to volunteer to be the tech guy on her Halloween fundraising project?

And why did he post *that* picture of her, on social media?

All Mindi wants is to focus on the Haunted House fundraiser she's coordinating to buy books for the new library at Beachside Elementary school. But Adam keeps getting in the way.

Game designer, Adam Kovac is thrilled to be back in his hometown of Hermosa Beach, and to get the old garage band back together again. He can't believe how much Dale's little cousin, Mindi has grown up since he last saw her, and how talented and creative she is.

But she won't give him the time of day. Especially since he posted that darn picture.

When Adam's technical skills are needed to make the Haunted House a success, will ghostly hauntings bring Mindi running into Adam's arms? Or send her straight into the arms of another?

**Coming Soon from Tari Lynn Jewett**

**Fascinator**

**Book One in the Secrets Never Die Series**

*She always did the right thing…until she didn't.*

It's 1928, born into California oil money, and a former Pasadena Rose Queen, Violet Conrad is beautiful, refined, and always follows the rules. Then on Friday, she witnesses her husband, Miles, in a compromising position and runs into an old high school friend from 'the wrong side of the tracks'.

Suddenly there are no rules.

But the other woman isn't Miles only secret, and now Violet has secrets of her own.

Who is Jack? And who has blood on their hands?

Fascinator is a story of repressed passion, greed, politics, love and redemption.

CPSIA information can be obtained
at www.ICGtesting.com
Printed in the USA
FSHW021829020619
58622FS

9 781733 594325